"Don't do that, Sam!"
said Mum.

"Eat your dinner, Sam!"
said Dad.

But Sam didn't want to.

Dad pretended the food
was a train.

"Choo, choo!" said Dad.
"Into the tunnel."

But Sam spat it out.

It went all over Dad's shirt.

"Please eat your dinner, Sam," said Jess. "Then you can have some ice cream."

But Sam didn't want to.

"Sam, you must eat your dinner," Mum said, "or Jasper will eat it all up!"

But Sam didn't want to.

Then Freddy ate some
of Sam's dinner.

"It's very good, Sam,"
said Freddy.

Sam's dinner was so good
that Freddy ate it all.
Sam was very cross.

"Dinner's ready!" said Mum.

But Freddy didn't want
his dinner. He wasn't
hungry anymore.

But Sam was!
He didn't want baby food.
He wanted Freddy's dinner.

START READING is a series of highly enjoyable books for beginner readers. They have been carefully graded to match the Book Bands widely used in schools. This enables readers to be sure they choose books that match their own reading ability.

The Bands are:

| Pink / Band 1 |
| Red / Band 2 |
| Yellow / Band 3 |
| Blue / Band 4 |
| Green / Band 5 |
| Orange / Band 6 |
| Turquoise / Band 7 |
| Purple / Band 8 |
| Gold / Band 9 |

START READING books can be read independently or shared with an adult. They promote the enjoyment of reading through satisfying stories supported by fun illustrations.

David Orme lives in Hampshire, England. He taught for 18 years before becoming a full-time writer. Recent books are on subjects as varied as dragons and how to be a pop star!

Beccy Blake started drawing family life when she was about Freddy's age, and has never really stopped since. Her Granny had a dog like the one in this story and Freddy is very much like her little brothers, getting up to all sorts of mischief!